GOING BUSH

KIRSTY GUNN

Going Bush

CENTER FOR WRITERS & TRANSLATORS
THE AMERICAN UNIVERSITY OF PARIS

—

SYLPH EDITIONS

At the end of the street where I lived, a street of gracious two-storey houses set in large gardens that were planted with oak and ash and maple, with English herbaceous borders and flowering fruit trees and shrubberies, was a park.

'A park?' you say.

A park, yes. But not a park as you know a park to be, not what you would call a park. It was the place where we went to play, at the end of our street.

This park was set with games areas for children as is the case with most parks, with railings around the green, and a swimming pool at the entrance. There was an avenue of magnolia trees that led from the front gate to the main picnic lawn. Places were set aside for different kinds of swings and slides, depending upon how adventurous you felt. Might it be the scary Witch's Hat? Or the spinner Carousel for babies? The long red and blue see-saw or the short yellow one? You choose. In summer you ran around in your swimming things, wet from the pool. You laid out your towel to dry in the hot sun and ate an ice cream from the little kiosk by the changing rooms that sold sweets and fizzy drinks.

But at the end of this 'green and pleasant land' was a thick pelt of New Zealand bush, starting at the border of the swings and slides where the smooth lawn finished, and spreading into the hills behind it – a dark presence waiting at the end of all the brightness and play. It clambered back up and over the rises and falls in the landscape behind the city, clogging gullies and ditches, stopping when the suburbs gave out to open farmland, paddocks – never 'fields' – but even then rising up again in pockets of thick growth, only really giving up when it reached the sea.

That bush ran in thick seams through the New Zealand of my childhood. It waited at the ends of roads, growing dense and dark at the edge of clusters of houses; it might be there when you turned a corner, a broad sunlit street giving way suddenly to a narrow track that was cut through the side of a hill. Certainly, our park could barely hold it back. The second playground – 'intermediate' it was called, where teenagers would never go although it had been created for grown-up children, with swings that went higher and a slide that was long and damaged with a frightening kink in the middle that could hurl you off halfway down – had bush growing right around it as though it were intended. It was dark and wet-smelling; half the things in it were rotting and the other half in bud. New Zealand bush does not have a season.

'Well, it's bush,' you say. 'Bush doesn't.'

It grows and dies and grows again – all at the same time, all through the year, scattering seeds and rotting, hosting worms and larvae and beetles even as it puts forth new shoots and brighter leaves.

'It's bush.'

Not woods. Not a forest. Nor a copse or a dell or a glade.

'It's bush. It doesn't translate.'

Perhaps it can change us, though?

'Change us?'

Perhaps.

After all, she could still hear the picnic, and see it, out of the corner of her eye, but with every step the girl was getting further and further from them. At one point, one of them called out: 'Girl! Don't you go too far! You be careful, hear? Stay close!' – but after that, nothing. There was a burst of laughter, raucous and yet dim, like she were listening to them through blankets, and though for a minute she'd stopped, just in case they were still watching, she knew she could walk on. She could go into the bush now if she wanted and she was going to; she was going to go right in. The heat... That was partly why she'd edged away, to find some relief from it, away from their bright picnic and their loud talking and songs, away from their picnic rugs and the boxes filled with beer and juice, their flasks of tea. Why did adults always have to make such a big fuss about everything, the girl had wondered earlier, when her mother and the aunts were unpacking the boxes and cooler bins they'd brought with them, the bags of swimming costumes and sun lotion and jerseys and towels. Why did they have to be like that? Be so busy? The girl had stood there, to one side, seeing them go backwards and forwards with their arms full. They were always packing and unpacking like that, she'd thought, making things to do for themselves when the weather was too hot to do anything but swim.

Her father had said in the car as they drove towards the park, 'Don't worry, there's bound to be a swimming pool there. You'll have fun with the rest of them...', meaning those paheka brothers and sisters of his, and his brother's children, her cousins. 'You will,' he'd told her, catching her eye in the rear-view mirror. The hot wind had entered through the open window, all yellow and green and the blue sky overhead and she'd wanted to close her eyes and laugh right into it. Instead, her father gave her a look again, and said, 'It will be good for you seeing your cousins again. These parks down here, they've got everything, swimming pools and tennis courts. Plenty of facilities. You will have a good time. You will.'

But when they arrived at the big park on the outskirts of town, there was no swimming pool, only swings and slides and a roundabout and she was too old for swing parks, she wasn't a baby. She was tall for her age, heavy and thick set, 'with a long torso' her mother said; the girl didn't know what a 'torso' was but it sounded like something rude. She had short strong legs, though, and strong legs were good. She knew that about herself, that she was strong, that there were things she could do that other girls couldn't, knew it like she knew other secrets about her body and how it was changing... Hair, blood, and no longer being flat beneath her singlet and cotton dresses but pushing out and growing there... Didn't her mother see? What was happening to her? Or did she not want to see? The girl was used to hiding from her mother at bath-times now, she hunched over when her parents talked to her so that she wouldn't seem so tall and strong. She drew her shoulders together when either of them came close, so the folds of her clothing might cover her body and all of her self that her mother said she should be careful not to show. 'Keep yourself covered up, hear me?' She nodded, mute, ashamed, ashamed of her mother's shame. It was this morning her mother had said that, with the blood coming and the terrible pains in her belly... 'Not another word,' she'd said, after she'd shown the girl what to do.

Because really, there's not another word for it. Only bush, bush everywhere here, and everywhere it stays the same – bush, just bush, collective and uncompromising. Neither singular nor plural, but both, resisting always the indefinite article that would make it some dainty shrub or hedge as well as the metonym that would have it stand for something larger. Bush. Bush. Bush. And it was growing, all this, at the edge of the 'park' at the end of our street. Look at what I've written in my notebook:

> *How can we have ever played here? How can we have made this place our home for childish games? The fort where we pretended we were Daniel Boone hiding from the Indians is pitch black inside and damp, and the pongas and flax that were planted to be like a garden around it have half grown up, have covered it with a sort of spoor and in the vegetation have bred wetas and huge spiders that rattle out from under the dead leaves when we go into the dark interior. Then, over here, is the little stream running down by the picnic green – we used to call it 'the burn', remember? That Scottish word for a little stream, how could we have called it that? – when, look at it! Choked with weeds and mud slick, water sluggish and engorged with rotting leaves... My brother tried to dam it, to create a pool to sail his boat, but no toy boats could sail there!*

'You make it seem like it was a terrible place, this park. You make it seem dangerous and unpleasant.'

And yet we did play there. We had walks. We had games, make-believe. We had tents, we made bows and arrows, we built shelters.

'But?'

Yes...

'You were frightened?'

Yes. It was terrifying there.

And she wasn't a baby. She wasn't. Her cousins, though, were teenagers, and older than her. Her parents had said that she would enjoy seeing them again, but the cousins were mean. The girl remembered, the minute she saw them. The boy picked at her clothes and the others stared and whispered. They mocked her silence. 'Listen to her, Terry!' said the oldest girl. 'Listen to what?' another one replied. 'There's nothing to listen to, dummy. She's a rock. Big things like that don't talk.' The cousin came up close to her, opened her mouth and closed it again, mouthing a silent word as though she were a frightening fish. 'She's like a maori-girl...Ain't ya?' the cousin said. 'Because I don't think she speaks at all.'

'Cut it out, Bethan!' the boy said then. 'You sound like white shit.' He took one of the girl's heavy plaits between his thumb and forefinger as if to measure it, weigh it. 'Anyhow, I like her,' he said. 'With her funny little country ways and her little itsy-bitsy dresses. And this hair-do here...' He ran his thumb and forefinger down the length of the plait while she stood, shock still, closing her eyes against him. 'I like it too.'

None of the adults heard, of course – and if they had? They would have laughed, or his mother would have cuffed Terry over the ears and he would have said, 'Hey, steady, Ma.' He would have smiled his bright white smile that made him look like a movie star. The older girl and the twins, they just stared at her mostly, with a fixed expression on their faces like: What kind of a thing are you?

'Does your mother make you wear your hair like that?' said one of them, after their brother had turned away. 'Cause it's really ugly.'

Maybe the dictionary can help: *'Bush: n. a woody plant in size between a tree and an undershrub.'* That's from the *Chambers 20th-Century Dictionary*, a British Dictionary with 'up-to-date English' as it states on the flyleaf, with 'everyday words'. And sure enough, right before us, here's the little British bush we all know so well, with its flowering leaves and dainty wooden branches, that 'woody plant'. But coming straight after, there it is: *'Bush: wild uncultivated country: such country covered with bushes; the wild. –v.i. to grow thick or bushy. –v.t. to set bushes about: to cover. adj. bushed, lost in the bush: bewildered.'*

And that word: *bewildered*...

Though, the girl thought, she herself, she knew, could never be lost there...

Even so, bewildered, yes.

But never lost there.

No. Never.

In the New Zealand of my childhood people used an expression within which was the nightmare of a place so overridden with *manuka* and scrub you might never escape it. This phrase, it seemed, existed permanently in a kind of future tense – that you might walk into and inhabit and be lost in: 'Going Bush'. My father used to say it, about a friend who'd made the decision to go into remote and difficult country, allowing himself to be altered by that experience. 'Ah yes, old Malcolm. He went bush in the end and you couldn't get much sense out of him by then.' As though, my father seemed to imply, by walking into that dense growth, a person would never afterwards be freed from it; changed forever. 'Poor old Malcolm wasn't good for anything after that,' my father said, 'he went bush, alright.' And friends of my parents would talk about it at parties, how they might go bush themselves – as a way of escaping from the easy daily routine, joking with each other about it, topping up their whiskies and laughing. The men saying that they might take a rifle in there and a fishing rod and think about never ever coming home again. 'That sounds just fine to me!' Or people would use the phrase at the beginning of the summer, as a way of describing how they were planning to relax, like they were 'going native', another expression that intimated the horror of an irreversible change. Women did not use this expression, they had no need. For them, in those days, there was no other life that might claim them – or that is what we children thought. They refreshed their lipstick and shook their heads when their husbands offered them another sherry. Only men went in there, into the Tarawheras or the Ureweras or the Kaimanawa Ranges. They came home, sun-blackened and with beards or stubble on their faces, laughing and smelling of earth and drink and something else – seeds or mould or blood.

 The girl remembered all of this, what the adults were like, what her cousins were like, the things they did and said, from last time, a long time ago when her parents had driven down South to meet her father's relations. Then, she'd been little and they had been tall. Now they were older but she was the tall one; she knew she was strong. Still, there were four of the cousins and only one of her. And how hot she was in the sun, in her dress that covered her up and the cardigan that went across her back like a rug. She wouldn't be able to run away from them like last time when she'd fled them to find her mother who had taken her by the hand and let her stay close. Now she would never be able to escape fast enough, not with the vest and dress and cardigan all stifling her like a heavy trap.

'Why doesn't she take all that ugly stuff off?' said the oldest girl, who was wearing a bikini and nothing else, and who kept running her thumb along the waistband low down on her belly. 'She must be baking, in all that stuff,' said another.

'She's cooking herself,' said the boy, and he caught the girl's eye and smiled.

'To be unobtainable,' my father tells me. 'Going Bush. That's what the expression means.'

Te Ara-A-Hongi: Hongi's Track.

Puketapu: Sacred hill or mound.

With roots, and mould, and spoor, and the tangle of new growth over everything, over any chance of a summer holiday at the beach, by a river or a lake.

Puarenga: The stream which flows through Whakarewarewa.

Te Puia: The burial hill at the edge of the geyser.

All keeping you in there, stopping you at the names of the places that were in the midst of all the growth.

Tarukenga: Place of slaughter.

Whakarewarewa: A place of uprising.

All bush, bush. The girl knows. How there at the edge of the bright sand, on the other side of the sparkling water, it was waiting for you.

Whangapipiro: Evil-smelling place.

When you swam to the other side of the bay where the water was in shadow, or turned a bend in the river and suddenly you were in deep.

Because she was country, the girl was. So country, her cousins said, that they couldn't understand a word her parents were saying. 'Did you hear the way he asked for a beer?' said the one called Bethan, talking about the girl's father. 'Like straight off the pa...'

'They're all maoris up there,' said the boy.

'They sure look that way,' said one of the twins, eyeing the girl as she stood, off to one side, trying not to see them, trying not to hear.

And all these landmarks, locations, these long site-words, naming-words, complex, reaching and growing words, all seeding

further meanings... *Te Ara-A-Hongi, Puketapu*... They had no meaning then, for me. Those words. The words that might break bush down, separate it, make of it this place here, or that place there. I didn't have the parts of speech, the articulations, pronunciations. I didn't have a way in, and bush gave, absolutely it gave, no quarter.

'Don't go in there again,' her mother had said. 'It's dangerous there, beyond the park where we're going.'

Because that dark would not be colonised by our games! We were little white children, little *Pakehas* the Maoris would have called us, lost in the midst of it: no synonym in English for the English noun that it devoured with its own reality.

Bush.

Just bush.

'Don't go in there,' her mother said.

That growth was everywhere, dense through my childhood and close and rotting – smelling, damp underfoot where the light couldn't reach the matted canopy of what we called, then, 'natives' – those trees indigenous to New Zealand, the *Matai* and the *Totara* and the *Miro* as I know to call them now – only, 'natives' we said then, because they were not oak or pine or ash. Those trees, too, grew unchecked, proliferating, vying for space and attention and the light of that blue, blue southern-hemisphere sky. The darkened air clanged with the sound of bellbird and *kea*. Wild pigs rooted amongst fallen branches and in the rotting trunks of giant *pongas*. The whole place alive with sound and rustling and the possibility of danger – but yes, we went in there, to play.

'You had to play there.'

Yes.

'All your games. Your Treasure Island and your Hide and Seek.'

Yes.

'Your Oranges and Lemons say the Bells of St Clement's.'

Yes.

'And Ring a Ring o' Roses and London Bridge is Falling Down.'

Yes and yes.

'You sang...'

In cotton dresses, drill shorts...

'With your pocket full of posies.'

In our pleated skirts and Fair-Isle cardigans sent to us from Scotland. Amidst the encroachment, the growth of *Kowhai-ngutu-kaka, Houi, Whauwhi, Piri-rangi* –

'You went in there.'

Yes.

'To play.'

And her mother had said that morning it was her fault, the blood. She'd been so frightened when she saw it in her pants, she'd thought she was going to die. 'Don't be so silly,' her mother had said. 'You big baby. It happens to every girl, so you'd better get used to it. Here –' and she'd taken her into the bathroom and closed the door. 'Now be quiet,' she said. 'And don't tell anyone about it, your father or anyone. And if the rest of them all go swimming today, you won't be able to. You'll have to say you don't want to.'

'What are you doing, you kids?' One of the uncles had broken away from the picnic and come over to the cousins, and stood, hands on his hips. 'Having fun? We're starting the barbecue in a minute. Go, all of you, and find some wood.' The cousins just looked at him: he wasn't their father, and after a minute of standing there and saying 'Well?' and no one replying, he turned, went back to where the rest of the adults were sitting on rugs and fold-out chairs.

'You're a perv, Terry,' said the oldest girl, when they were alone again. 'Stop looking at her, she's just a little kid.'

'She's big though, eh?' one of the younger ones said. 'She's all... developed and everything. And look at those legs. Christ, she could play rugby for King Country.'

The girl turned then, her eyes stinging with tears. There was nothing she could do. Her parents might as well be in another park, at another picnic; they were laughing and talking. And her mother was still angry with her, from this morning it seemed, so she couldn't go to her now and put her head in her lap like she used to do. She heard the cousins laughing, behind her back, the adults laughing too.

She waited for a while, not moving, and then, when the barbecue was lit and the men were gathered round, talking and making jokes, when the flames of the fire were playing under the barbecue grill and even the cousins were moving towards it, that's when she'd started walking away from them, her face hot and scalded, her heart thumping with fear that they would see her and come and fetch her. For a second she looked back, to where by now they were all seated on the rugs, around them the food her mother had made, really fancy food, and they were starting to eat that, the tubs of coleslaw and the roast chicken and the bread with a hole cut out and stuffed with ham and lettuce and egg. And there were bottles of pop from the shops, not orangeade but real Fanta and Coke – she saw the cousins divide them out and use the bottle opener. She pressed her lips together, she was so thirsty. But there would be water to drink where she was going, she would find it. There would be water to swim in, too. Wairoa. Waimangu.

Soon, her father would take out his guitar and start to sing, and the minute she'd seen him go to the boot of the car for the guitar case and more drinks, she knew she could slip away. By then the cousins, too, were joking with their parents, and with her parents, and the aunts and uncles who had no children. The boy had persuaded his father to give him a beer, and he'd already drunk most of the bottle; the girl had seen him do that, in one long swallow, lying back along the side of his parents' car. One of his sisters had gone over to him, poking his bare stomach with the point of her toe.

'Hey, naughty boy,' she'd said.

For holidays and long weekends, when I was a child, we went to the Wairarapa, where my mother's family had lived ever since my grandmother's grandfather had arrived on the first ships to New Zealand out of Ullapool, on the north-west coast of Scotland. This was farming country – over the Rimatuka hills you came – and the land was laid out, flat and rolling gently into pastures and paddocks, orchards and vales. Villages, small market towns as we might call them in Britain, dotted the landscape, maple and oak and flowering apple and plum had been planted in rows or next to old farmhouses. There were hills, but they were yellow and sheep-bitten in the summer, tending to gorse and scree.

On one of her trips into just such country, Katherine Mansfield kept a diary – her 'Urewera Notebook'. She was only a girl, and this was a long camping holiday that took her into the very centre of New Zealand's North Island, a little north of the Wairarapa but into that same kind of country, with its bare expanses, its paddocks, its cabbage trees, its thick depths of *manuka* and *houhere* and *whauwhau*:

> *The manuka and sheep country – very steep and bare – yet relieved here and there by rivers and willows – and bush ravines... Tuesday morning start very early – Titi-o-Kura – the rough road and glorious mountains and bush – The top of Taranga-kuma – rain in the morning – then a clear day – the view – mountains all round... We lunch past the Maori pa and get right into the bush.*

Mansfield calls it 'the middle of the country': the landscape of the Ureweras, like the Wairarapa, wild and lonely where there's plenty of space for grazing, plenty of land that's bare and bony from standing in so much light. Yet, even so, there at the base of an escarpment – at the edge of my grandmother's 'village', as we never called it – is a river, and bush is all around it. Because originally, before the farms, before the sheep, it would have been all bush here. In my notebook I write:

> *When we came back to the Wairarapa, in midwinter, in the cold, we could see how the darkness of the growth around the river seemed to cast shadows that reached even as far as Nanna's little wooden house up on the hill. Like an underpainting, a ground, a sub-colour, a pigment of wet green and black, green black of leaves, black mud. Even through the pastel and sorbet shades of Nanna's roses that used to pile in a massed tumble over the white painted fence in her garden how the dark smears of that other palette must have blotched the pale petals. How, in the midst of summer, even, within the tangle of the pale pink and lemon blooms was there the shade of the gully at the bottom of her garden. She brought goats in one year to clear that part for vegetables – is what she said the goats were there for, goats and pigs clear off the bush, some people say. And did they clear it? They cleared a section – I remember the silver beet and kumera and 'taters' as she called them, that she grew there in that patch of squared off earth past the edges of her garden. But below the tidy arrangement of earth and vegetable garden was the gully just the same.*

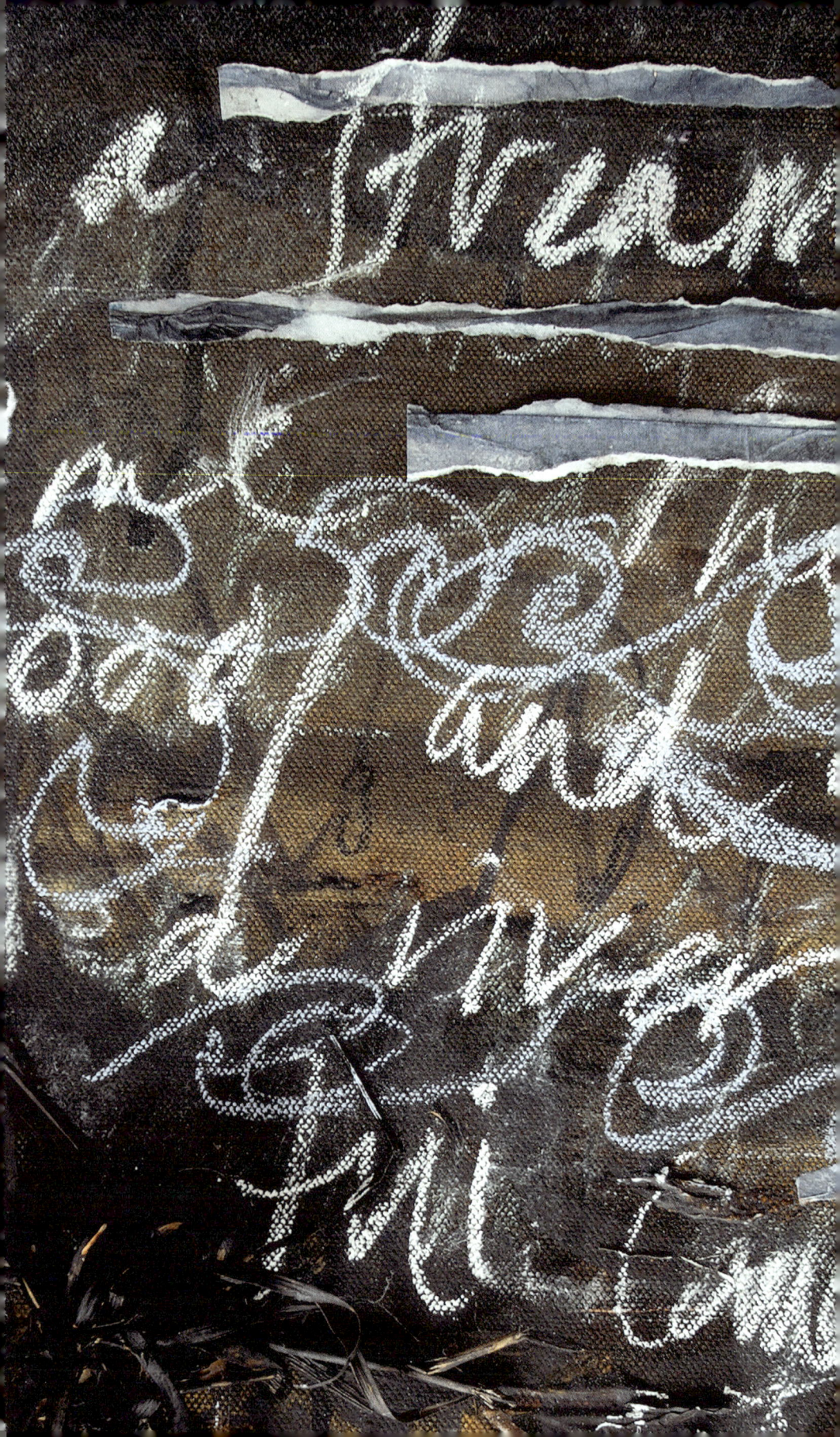

'So this is real countryside, yes? We're deep in the country now, in "the middle" of it, as Mansfield said?'

Except we didn't say 'countryside'. We said... What did we say? We said we were 'headed North'. That was the New Zealand thing to say. My mother said it, 'Headed North. Going Home'. We children said, 'Going up to Nanna's', or 'Up Country'. Or 'Going to the country'.

'Because the country as place of leisure. A 'Locus Amoenae'. A rural idyll or pastoral...'

That 'country' didn't translate.

'No, no, don't touch me,' my mother cried out to my father when he returned from one of his own forays into bush, away with his man-friends for days at a time – 'And what were they doing in there?' my grandmother used to ask me. 'What did they think they were doing? They stink to high heaven.' They had driven out into it in a battered up old ute, and one of them had killed something while they'd been in there, I saw it out by the tailgate, wrapped in a canvas sack.

'So "real countryside", yes. I see what you mean.'

But this was no kind of 'countryside' at all.

'I see exactly what you mean.'

And by now the girl had been able to start walking away, because no one had been talking to her then, or plucking at her cardigan and saying, 'What are you hiding under there?' Walking backwards at first so it seemed like she was still there with them, and only once had they called out. She could still hear them, through the blanket of her privacy – there was the far strike of a guitar, a surge of distant laughter – but by now she was where she had been told not to go, where there'd be no paths, no way in or out.

Because there are no paths, no ways...

'I do see, yes... No maps, no routes to follow, no way to place your going in, your coming out.'

Exactly. For example, at the base of the ridge that one could see from my grandmother's kitchen window was a long thick strip of dark green where the river was, a place we were drawn to over and over.

'To picnic? Swim?'

Well, it might have looked that way. Certainly we took things to make a fire, to camp out.

'But –'

Something was wrong. Apart from the darkness, I mean, and the smell, the lack of sun. The wet underfoot that meant camping was uncomfortable and we got clammy and damp.

'It was wrong?'

A transgression... Was how it felt. To try and make of this place a woodland glade, or a dell. A picnic spot. To make of this gully by the slow-moving slip of green water that slid underfoot with muds and with knots of eels set into the banks... To transplant ourselves there, the little *pakehas* thinking they could make themselves at home... To think we could have our Scottish picnic in the dark! With our flask of tea and cake and our orangeade. To think that we might try and fashion from our British books about adventures a place in that dark that would accommodate us! That we might – what? Have reflected back to us in the shadows and undergrowth the bright pages of our Scottish Annuals and our Puffin paperbacks?

Katherine Mansfield writes:

> *From this saddle we look across river upon river of green bush then burnt bush russet colour – blue distance... At the head of a great valley the blazing sun uplifts – like a giant torch to light the bush – and even in the bright sunlight it is still so passionately secret... the green place in vivid sunlight and the silent and green bush...*

She tries, as though she could, to translate: 'green place', 'great valley', 'blazing sun'; all these words she imports to the place to give it meaning, locate it, limit it. As though anyone could, when, from the North to the South Island, from the east to the west coast, into the high gorges in the ranges and to the edge of the sea, bush covered the country and always kept its secrets, its lost lakes and rivers, caves and cataracts, geysers, mudpools, and boiling waters. All the true names were secret then, all the colours of *aniwaniwa*, the earthy slices of *ruawahia*, inky depths of *waimangu*, hidden far from that light, her 'blazing sun'.

'I am *so* happy,' Mansfield writes, from deep, deep within her native country. 'The sweetness –' *the sweetness* – 'of this wild place...'

'It's dangerous there,' the girl's mother had said, as they were driving this morning. 'Remember what happened last time you went into somewhere like that, and we couldn't find you. We don't want that happening again. So don't you even think about it. Stay on the lawn of the park where we can see you. You be good.'

The girl had nodded. She did remember last time, though it was long ago; she remembered how angry her parents had been. It had been dark in there, in the forbidden place hidden from the children who had gathered around her in the school playground and frightened her. But she had left them all, their faces coming up close to her and their loud voices, and she had been safe, she had been safe, hadn't she? She'd been safe in there and not lost at all.

So, yes, she'd nodded to her mother, but it had been all she'd been thinking about since the picnic had started – in the hot sun, with her grown-up cousins' eyes upon her, the girls' wrinkled noses going, 'Ugh, can you smell something here? Like someone's got their period or something...' Going one to the other, 'You smell that too?' That day long ago she had put stones in her pockets that she'd found, and she'd had a branch that she'd wanted to use against the children if they'd chased her. Her mother had been angry about that too. She'd been angry about the stones and the branch, angry about everything. But why be angry, the girl thought now? Wasn't that just like being busy at the picnic, unpacking boxes all the time and being cross and tired?

Because now, the girl thought, that she was this close, with the hot sun on her head, everything in there looked dark and cool, the whole of it a place of shadow and so easy to be in there, with nothing to worry or be angry about. And if she could just get far enough, deep enough, in... Then they wouldn't find her like they had before. She wouldn't have to worry that they might come after her, and this time she could stay. She stood at the edge of it, caught its dark earth odours for the second before it seemed to part like an opening seam, the soft split of foliage allowing her to enter – and in that same second, across the lawn, where the cars were parked and her family were gathered, one of them, the oldest cousin, lifted his head from the bottle he balanced between his thighs and saw her, this heavy girl-woman with her big legs and her silent Maori ways, at the edge of the park, saw her, hesitating... Then she was gone.

I kept my own journal when I returned to these places of my New Zealand childhood. I made records, took photographs, wrote stories out of the leaves and trees and rivers that I saw; by then I had species and place names for some of them, a dictionary of plants and flowers. But this – my 'Wairarapa Notebook' – was no country log, no countrywoman's diary. It was my own little secret, my booklet of strange words, filled with *kowhai* and *horoeka* and *kauri*. The thin pages were crammed with the sort of vegetation that one could never press within the leaves of a journal. Here were no bluebells. No cowslip. My grandmother's garden, when I saw it again, after all the years that had passed, was overrun with flax and *toi toi*, and the veranda was broken and in shadow.

'*Where am I?*' I wrote.

In that part of the country that was no 'country', with its 'villages' of Pahiatua and Eketahuna and Wairau set within the folds of the hills... Where was I, that I could barely know myself in these places, as if I'd never known them? Yet all the information, the colours and the smells, seemed to have proofed themselves, held fast across the years. Still I had written 'Country Journal' on the cover of my notebook, this book of strange names and plants and places where summer is winter and sunlight means dark. I persisted, as if writing itself might help me understand, as if I could find my way backwards – in words. Writing about grasses and odours and the touch of wet earth, the fur of the *ponga's* bark. Writing about the smell of the rain and the white slugs of weta larvae that came burrowing out of the roots when the torrent had passed. Writing in a secret book about a place that had once been my...

'Yes?'

Once been my...

'Yes?'

My home.

When I saw the Wairarapa again after all the years, and I went back to that long-lost river, when I took off my shoes and waded in:

> *No 'Highland river', this, so slow and secretive and deep, in the bottom of the gully: it has been waiting for me here. My own Highland river back in Sutherland is laid out like a scarf through the strath, it sits high on the land, breaking and scattering over*

rocks in spate, furled at its blue-black edges with foam and cold. The pale grass spreads out from either side of that river. Where this one hides itself, slides deep in the cut of the bank and makes no sound... We used to take inner-tubes from tyres and drift downstream while the adults hunched on the banks and tried to rouse a fire to cook sausages and boil water for tea. We sang 'The Rowan Tree' and 'Flow Gently Sweet Afton' while the trees pressed in around us, and we shivered after leaving the water. Only my brother, with his skin burned dark by the New Zealand summer sun, who'd found high rocks to dive from and caught eels on string with a nail for a hook – only he seemed as if he might have belonged there. Like a little Maori boy, with his bony brown body springing into the water and disappearing into its depths, holding his breath and staying under, like an eel himself amongst the mud and boulders. The rest of us, pale in our cotton shorts and floral dresses – what were we doing there? It was midsummer and we were shivering, emerging from the shallows. There was no sun to be seen there. Was it summer at all?

Still, the writing down, the recording of places, colours, textures... I persisted.

'Though New Zealand bush has no season, though it dies and grows at the same time...'

Still, I wrote down the feeling of being there, within it.

'While it scatters seeds and rots as you walk through it. While insects and flying things nest in it as it's decomposing.'

I persisted. My writing...

'It was your own way –'

Yes. Of going in there, and staying.

'Yes.'

Though I didn't know the proper names of anything that grew.

'You knew what bush was.'

I did. I remembered.

And yes, she heard herself now, saying that word.

Yes, she said.

Stay now, then, girl, and continue: for there, back in the writing, is that list that was made:

Houhere – Lace Bark, Ribbon Wood, Houi, Whauwhi.

Rata – Red Misletoe, Piri-rangi.

Miro.

Ngaio.

All the words from the places of childhood. The holidays, excursions:

Rotowhero,

Orakei-Korako.

All the places you went into, in the dark:

Huka Falls,

Horohoro,

Maunga-Kakaramea.

Write them down now in the secret book, the letters making lakes and foamy water, warm springs, and mirror pools, twisting into plants, trees, all the different shapes and sounds of the language that are the foliage and branches and berries and stalks:

Kaka Beak,

Matai,

Rewarewa.

Write the letters down as if they might turn into words that in turn would make more words, leaf by leaf, stream by stream: make up that one word, bush, that in turn becomes Wairarapa and Urewera and Rimutuka...

Kowhai,

Horoeka,

Little Mingimingi.

These names with their twisting and clinging consonants and hyphens and their syllables repeating vowels deep, deep in bush:

Huritini: Ever circling, or many circles; the large pool of boiling muddy water at *Tikitere*: Drifting carved image.

Tu Moana: Standing in the lake.

Pae-Hinahina: Headland or ridge clothed with *hinahina* or *mahoe* trees.

Tapuwae-Harururu: Resounding footsteps, the name of a beach, a village.

Okataina: The place of laughing.

Wai-Kimihia: The water sought.

And water found. Because once inside, all changed for the girl. Her body was like a gleam, like a pale light in the interior that thickened and closed around her, held her. With the coolness came the idea that she herself might be part of it; she could smell water, somewhere close. She took a deep breath... Clean and deep and cool. It might be just over there, she thought, right there, in there... A lovely river, for coolness, for swimming, deep and fast, and though the great towel her mother had pressed between her legs reminded her that she should not take off her clothes, she did, removed her cardigan, then her sandals. At once she felt so light it was as though someone had lifted her right up, as though she could fly! She took a few steps, light, light steps, then stopped, unbuttoned her dress, let it fall from her to the ground. Now, just wearing her vest and pants, she could start to run...

And, yes.

She heard herself saying the word, as she started running.

Yes.

Because she was strong and because she was fast.

Yes, she said.

Wai-Kimihia.

Yes and yes and yes.

A little *kowhai* flower turned to paper when I placed it between tissue and weighted it with three dictionaries – the Oxford, the Webster, and the Chambers. The heft of all the English words laid down upon a small pale lemon bell-shaped flower and its strand of stamens and stem...

And see how the long soft ferns wanted to be close to her, touching her, brushing her arms as she ran to find the river, and the vines wanting to clasp her legs but letting her go just as easy.

Yes, she said again. And yes.

See how each piece of the flower – each fragment, each single word – carries its own world within it.

Yes, and yes.

For now she was running faster and faster. The soft clay and dust floor was powdery and cool under the soles of her feet. Though the undergrowth was thick and dark, it wanted her to be inside it, wanted her to run faster and faster to find its secret river, to touch her and hold her and whisper and call, along with the bellbirds and tuis and fantails she could hear, somewhere up there, in the dark trees, flitting in and out of the dark branches like ghost birds and spirits of ancestors with their calls like the sounds of bells: Come to me, come to me, come to me.

There's a river, said a tui, come to me, said the river.

There's a pool, said the river, come to me.
There's a stream, said the pool, and a waterfall...come.
There's a river, said the tui, come to me, said the river.

Because it would be just ahead of her, she knew, the run of water, the river's muds and slides, its cool flank, just beyond her, just there, in there, somewhere in the dark. She'd stopped running, was panting, her arms wrapped fully around the trunk of a large ponga fern, its fronds a canopy over her head, as though she were part of its growth, part of its stature. She wrapped her arms tighter, tighter, hearing the song complete now, the bush calling to her, 'Come to me,' and singing – and she smiled. All that time ago, when she'd run away, before they'd found her, the bush had looked after her then like now, held her and let itself be held, sang her songs, let her hear its own talking. She hadn't felt heavy then, or encumbered by clothes, bound up like the tightly wound plaits that her mother fixed into her hair each day. Just as she'd done then, she now loosened her hair, one hank of plait at a time, this one, that one... She put her fingers through it all, through all her long hair, teasing out the twisted strands, then took off the last of her clothes, the cotton vest with the straps that cut into the tops of her arms and held her in so tight she felt she couldn't breathe, the pants with their thing inside that her mother had pinned there. She ran a few yards more and there in front of her, she was standing on its bank, was the river. A glint of sun illuminated its water, gold, gold green, gold brown, gold brown and gold. Then she stepped off the bank and into it, the current took her, and she was down...

And yes, again, she heard the lovely word.
And yes.
And, one-two, she held her breath and then released it, coming up to the surface and floating now, light as water, while green and gold painted over her whiteness, made of her something small, quiet and lonely and unafraid.
All water.
She took another breath, one-two, one-two, going under again and coming up again, all air and water and river.
All yes.
And down again, she held her breath, went deep down...
One-two.

And up again.
Yes.
Took a breath.
Then there was a cry. 'She's in here!'
And her breathing stopped.

I went back to my notebook, to remember all the places we'd seen, the country, the feel of it. I was trying to remember, to start thinking how I might write about this, the country I was born into, the dark places it held and what they might mean. Under the heading 'Visit to Mount Bruce', I wrote:

> *It does not smell like an English wood. Or a Scottish forest. It does not smell like a copse or a glade or a dell. No scent of flowers or animals. I can not find any similes for the experience of being in amongst this growth, this overgrowth, undergrowth. I can not see the sky when we walk down into the gully that hides a river. I can not –*

I remember the notices that had been put on the bark of the trees in that wildlife sanctuary with its Scottish name: '*Miro*', '*Ngaio*', I'd written, under 'Visit to Mount Bruce'. I heard voices in the bush and the shrieking of the *keas* being fed.

'Come inside,' the voices said.

They were right there – she could hear them – across the water.

'The dirty whore, she's taken off her clothes!' There were the cries of them now coming through the bush, and their ringing laughter.

'She's in here somewhere! You're in here, ain't you?' And the sound then of them coming after her, getting closer.

'Hinemoa?' the boy called out. 'You hear me? We're going to get you now, you naughty, naughty girl.'

Quick, whispered the water.

The girl scrambled up to the side of the river, slipped, fell back. She couldn't catch her footing, went under, panicked, came up gasping for breath.

'Please help me!' she cried out to the bush.

'You hear that?' In the distance, but closer than before.

'I didn't think Hinemoa could talk,' someone said, someone near.

'Hinemoa was a maori princess, dummy. This one's no princess, she's a dumb whore.'

'C'mon, then!'

They were all very near. Though they had not seen her they were right there.

'Let's get her! This way!'

'Help me!' the girl screamed again, and this time managed to hold on to a rock and pull herself out of the water, lift herself, all her nakedness, onto the wet bank.

'Be careful,' said the river. Then: 'I can help you.'

'And listen,' said the bush, 'I will tell you what to do.'

But she was crying, couldn't see. Her heart was giving out a great drumbeat of sound.

'Shhh,' said the river. 'Listen...'

See what's waiting for you here:

Whauwhau tree, up to eight metres tall, leaves palmate, stalked, toothed, with thick dark-green glossy midrib and light green veins.

Titoki, reaching upwards with branchlets, and leafstalks brown furred.

Mingimingi. Bark black. Leaves showing parallel veins. Flowers and fruit arranged in bundles.

Horoeka, an unbranched stem with long lance-shaped leaves, dark green matt.

Ngaio.

Manuka.

Totara. Leaves dark green, darker, dark...

All bush but different, separate:

Miro.

Rimu.

Each part its own, each leaf and twig distinct:

Piri-rangi.

Tawhai.

Come inside, they say.

Houi.

Whauwhi.

Come inside, each consonant, each vowel and syllable...

Rewarewa.

Houhere.

Come inside, the words are saying. Though there are no paths, no way in, or out...

Come inside, they say. Come inside.

'Use me,' said the river bank, 'and me,' the bush whispered, 'and me' – the bush floor. 'Come inside,' they whispered, and stay.

And the girl leaned over then, lifted great handfuls of the dark soft clay of the riverbank and – quickly quickly – she smeared it over her skin, hearing her own panting, her own enormous heart. Great handfuls of the dark mud she scooped up and used it to coat her belly and thighs, paint her arms, her buttocks, her breasts, and her throat... Quickly quickly... All over her went the mud. 'Use me,' said the riverbank again, 'and me,' said the bush, as she broke off a huge piece of log, half rotten but enormous, from the tree beside the river, put it up like the post of a fence before her. 'And me,' said the bush floor, as she took up a handful of its dark fibres and dust and spread that too across her body, and then more mud, on her face, coating herself, before she heard, very close now –

'Look at this! What she's done!'

They weren't calling out now.

'The dirty animal, that makes me sick.'

They were so close she could hear their low voices.

'She's disgusting,' one of them said. 'Leaving it there for everyone to see.'

By now the girl was silent, by the tree, behind the tree branch that she held. 'Don't move,' the tree said, the great totara, its trunk next to her. 'Stand with me,' said the tree. 'And don't make a sound.'

'She's nearby,' said the boy cousin. 'I know it.'

'I can smell her,' said another.

'Let's get her,' the boy said, like a hunter, like a man. 'C'mon!'

And she heard them running then, down the side of the river, and she saw them, their shapes coming through the dark, closer and closer. They were whooping, 'We can smell you! We can see you!'

But still she did not move; she stood dark and silent as the tree that protected her, while they ran straight past her and into the bush, unseeing, deeper and deeper in, their whiteness rushing past her body covered with mud and ponga dust and earth, ground deep into her skin.

'Where's she gone?' she heard them calling, the colours of her dark brown and black and green, making even of the slide of blood that ran down the inside of her leg the same dark shade, and of her long heavy hair that fell down her back like hanks of soft bark, and of her arms that were like branches and of her fingers and hands that could have been roots and vines. So she stood as they came for her, and went past her, brushing against her unseeing.

'I know she's in here!' she heard one of them cry out, though already their voices sounded distant.

'We'll find her!' she heard, but barely. 'We'll get her...'

The girl closed her eyes and waited. If they came back, it would be like that time long ago, when they'd found her and taken her away from where she'd been hidden – and that time she'd had only stones and a branch...

This time – she lifted it – she had a piece of tree and in her other hand a boulder loosened from the river bank when she'd been scrambling up out of the water, stricken with fear and unable to breathe.

'Use me,' the river bank had told her then. It had said the same again as she had stood there like a mighty tree, dark and silent, while the terrible cousins ran straight on past her – and she had let them go.

COLOPHON

THE CAHIERS SERIES · NUMBER 27
ISBN: 978-1-909631-17-5

Printed by Principal Colour, Paddock Wood, on Neptune Unique (text) and Chagall (dust jacket). Set in Giovanni Mardersteig's Monotype Dante.

Series Editor: Dan Gunn
Associate Series Editor: Daniel Medin
Design: Sylph Editions Design

Text: ©Kirsty Gunn, 2016
Installation: ©Merran Gunn, 2016
    photographed by Fergus Mather

With thanks to Marie Donnelly, and to the the San Francisco Foundation, for their generous support.

No part of this publication may be reproduced in any form whatsoever without the prior permission of the author or the publishers.

CENTER FOR WRITERS & TRANSLATORS
THE AMERICAN UNIVERSITY OF PARIS

SYLPH EDITIONS, LONDON | 2016

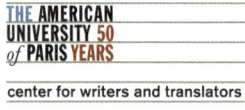

www.aup.edu · www.sylpheditions.com